The story's beginning. . .

and the moon's flying high. . .

trailing fat clouds across the night sky.

. . . and creep. . .

I'm a thing

that goes

BUMP

in the night.

out of the door,

past the gate . . .

through the deep summer grasses
at the edge of the lawn,
to the place where we gather
to dance until dawn.

And here is the hill where
the wide awake meet,

in jim-jams and slippers
and some with bare feet.

There is music and laughter drifting up from the trees,

as we dance in the sky with the owls and the bees . . .

over oceans and mountains,
across rivers and streams,

we dance to a lullaby
deep in our dreams.

But we're starting to yawn and beginning to wilt,

So . . .
we're flying
back home
to where
somebody cares,
falling into
our pillows,
tightly hugging
our bears.

Now here comes
my someone who
goes HUG in the night . . .

kisses me gently,